T.M. Cooks is the p⸱   ⸱ ⸱ol-
laborative writing tea⸱ ⸱ ⸱ ⸱ne contributors are;

- Pippa Church

- Brendan Davies

- Sue Moffat

- Rachel Reddihough

- Julianna Skarzynska

with cover design by Julianna Skarzynska. The cover uses:

A personal picture by Julianna Skarzynska

A picture of Bottle Ovens by Ed Chadwick

Vectorized silhouettes of Hansel and Gretel by Immanuel Giel

Derivative work by Collin Knopp-Schwyn

The project was overseen by Dr Yvonne Skipper.

The group cheerfully acknowledges the wonderful help given by:

- Keele University and White Waters Writers for this wonderful opportunity to collaborate and create, for sharing their methodologies and supporting us through the process of writing this book.

- Dr Yvonne Skipper

- Joe Reddington

- Phoebe Gill

It's been a wonderful opportunity, and everyone involved has been filled with incredible knowledge and enthusiasm.

The group of five practitioners from the New Vic Borderlines started to plan out their novel at 12.00 on Wednesday 20th September 2017 and completed their last proofreading at 17.00 on Friday 22nd September (19hrs of work).

We are incredibly proud to state that every word of the story, every idea, every chapter and yes, every mistake, is entirely their own work. Any errors you do find please take pleasure in, enjoy, mock, and scold as you wish.

We would happily receive copies of the book engraved in red biro at your displeasure.

We are sure you will agree that this is an incredible achievement.

Grimm State of Mind

T. M. Cooks

Contents

Chapter 1

The Stage is Set

It was only Wednesday, and far too early to be walking down the street, especially when it was half-term... and just to make this day even better it was raining you know the kind of rain that hurts your skin, dripping from the kind of sky that looks like it has been grey forever. Damon wished that he had never thrown that chair across

the room at Mr Frobshaw (the drama teacher-
the sort of drama teacher that everyone
wanted to have as their from tutor), and
even to this day he had no idea how it
managed to stop mid air and turn an almost perfect right-angle away from his tar-
get straight through the plate-glass window. His form had been very privileged'
to take part in an all day drama workshop
at the local theatre because Mr Frobshaw
had been to university with the director,
Anthony. Why couldn't people just leave
him alone? He'd told them he didn't want
to play the stupid game so they should
just have respected him that's the trouble
with teachers these days, they've got no
respect. The worst thing was the laughter, that's what made him snap. Damon
felt like he was always being laughed at

and it was never the kind of nice laughter where everyone is joining in, the having a laugh' kind of laughter, but the cold sneering kind of laughter that's cruel and cutting. Damon had become an expert at being cruel and cutting, always making sure he got his retaliation in first, he particularly liked directing it towards the smart alec kids, or the teachers. He never used it against the quiet kids or the losers because that would be mean and Damon did not believe he was mean, he just was not going to be laughed at. As he turned onto the High Street he wished that he'd just been cruel and cutting to Mr Frobshaw that day, the worst that would have happened would have been detention, but instead of clever words he found himself reaching over and taking the back of the chair in both his hands. As he walked past the Wrights pie shop Damon was sure that he just saw two workmen splat' each other in the face, but as he was about to take a second look, a car horn aggressively screamed at him. Damon gesticulated appropriately

Inside the car, Mr and Mrs Bevan were shocked when a young lad walked out in front of the car.

"I can't bear it when you use the horn, there's no need to you nearly scared the life out of that poor boy."

"He was about to step right out in front of me, he should have been paying attention For gordon's sake, he's got that hood pulled so far down over his head I'm surprised he can even see And could anyone please tell me why you would wear a cap and a hood. What kind of statement about yourself is that making to the world?"

Mr and Mrs Bevan continued to contemplate the state of kids, the world, the stock exchange and the weather. Their disgruntled mutterings merged into the constant drone of the windscreen wipers.

Patricia turned to her brother and said "I'm sure that was Damon we should have stopped and offered him a lift...he's going to be soaked by the time he gets to the theatre"

"There's no way dad would have stoppedyou know what he's like "I'm damn well late already, do you know what it looks like when a barrister turns up late to court it doesn't look good I can tell you." Delius did a perfect impression of his father including his deeply serious knitted brows which told the kids "do not distract me I am a very busy man'. "Anyway I bet Damon wouldn't want to have a lift with us

"Why not?" Patricia sounded slightly wounded by this suggestion, as if there could be something wrong with such a simple offer, a sensible offer, a generous and kind offer. The thought of Damon refusing to accept a lift from her made her feel unreasonably angry towards him. She turned on her brother and reminded him "And you shouldn't have told him you are only eleven, you're supposed to be thirteen for this half-term project if you get chucked off because you're too young, mum and dad will go mad"

The car stopped at the traffic lights. Delius peered through the window at the bus which had stopped next to them. The red-light raindrops ran down the panes of glass. Delius saw they left little trails of turquoise moving down the glass like strange tadpoles.

* * *

Dylan banged on the closed doors of the bus. The driver ignored him at first and then had a change of heart and opened the door. "I'm only supposed to let people get on at the bus-stops you'll get me sacked." The lights changed to amber and they began to move. There was an empty seat half way down the bus next to a large lady with a child on her knee. Just as Dylan was about to sit down a very lanky man with a pony-tail, who had been sitting in the seat opposite, neatly slid into the seat right under his nose. Dylan turned to the man's now vacant seat and went to sit there, a small man with a huge beard ran and sprang into it from a seat near the back of the bus. Dylan made his way to the back and there in front of him was the large lady complete with child on her lap. He turned to move back down the bus again only to see that each of the passengers seemed to moving around the seats. It reminded him oddly of one of the weird games he had been playing at the theatre. Dylan was really not in the mood. He decided to just stand. The greyness of the sky suited him perfectly today, it seemed to him that there was no colour in the world anymore. He allowed the words to form in his mind. "Mum is dying."

* * *

"The great thing about riding a bike

is it means you can get about, go anywhere, weave in and out of stopped cars,
you're free!" As usual Doris was having
a great conversation with herself as yet
again she put on a brave face, this time
turning this hideous cold wet grey jour-
ney... on a bike... in October... without
any waterproofs, into a bid for freedom.
Actually nothing could dampen her spir-
its, because today they would all find out
which role they were going to play in the
theatre's production of Hansel and Gretel.
She had never had the opportunity to per-
form before because the only drama that
happened during term time was always after school and Doris was a busy girl. In re-
ality she was a young-carer, but like many
young carers nobody notices what she did,
only that sometimes she didn't have her

homework or her gym kit, and that sometimes it looks like she's wearing the same
clothes as yesterday (because she is). But
mostly they notice that she never meets
up after school or goes to anyone's house
for sleep overs. I really really want to
be Gretel . Don't be stupid. Gretel's a
smart girl and pretty too Patricia should
play Gretel she'll be perfect. Oh gosh I
hope i'm not the witch I'm really scared
of witches Fifteen years old and still scared
of witches! Perhaps I can be a woodland
creature or something.' Her mood turned
from excited to anxious. She turned off
Victoria Road and straight past Damon,
riding through a huge puddle and literally
drenching him. "Oh no I'm so sorry, " she
said.

Damon glowered at her "It's ok, " he

said.

Chapter 2

Over Casting

One by one the space filled, Dylan found himself a corner to hide against, hood up, eyes down, willing no one to notice him. He could hear Trish or Dish' as she was now being referred to chatting nervously to Delius who didn't appear to be paying attention.

"I hope I'm not the witch - she is not

very bright - fancy falling for that trick with the bones!"

Dylan glanced across the room Anthony was muttering in the corner looking fretful over his script.

Alex was looking over Anthony's shoulder, he was dressed in black, the traditional dress of a technician. Wrapped around him was a long dark cloak, he liked the way that the cloak felt. He found it on a hook in the house. Anthony was worried, he always was, always had been since it happened. A feeling of guilt washed over him. He looked again at Anthony's script. "Here we go again, " he thought.

Damon was outside, Dylan could see him from the window having his last shifty fag before rehearsals started. Doris appeared in the doorway.

"Morning!" She chirped "I'm so excited about today!"

The strange things they had noticed that morning were totally forgotten about.

"Alex, who do I give this role to? I can't find the right person for it." Anthony scratched his head.

Alex moved through the space, hovering by each of the children for a second before stopping at Dylan.

"That's what I thought, but I don't think he is up for it? He doesn't want to be here, does he?" Anthony looked back at the lists of names he had scribbled out and rewritten. "But he is the only one the character fits."

Alex moved closer to Dylan, looking closely at the boy who desperately wanted to be anywhere but there. Dylan looked up and saw Anthony staring intently at him.

"Right everyone, circle up!" Anthony called.

The group individually grabbed a chair and moved them into the middle of the room, forming a large circle. Trish was the first one there, she sat with the script on her lap and a highlighter pen in hand.

"After much deliberation I have assigned roles for you all - in no particular order; Dad will be played by Delius"

Delius shrugged, neither happy or sad about this information.

"Mum - Patricia, sorry - Trish, " Anthony corrected himself

"Its Dish now Anthony" Damon smirked. "All the Ds together remember!" The others laughed.

Trish looked down, trying to blink the

tears out of her eyes. I'm the mother? That's an awful role, ' she thought. She looked over at Damon who was still chuckling to himself I thought they would have forgotten about that Dish thing by now.' They had been playing name games on the first day, most of the group had names beginning with D, Delius had found himself all tongue tied mid game and called out "Dish Dish Dish!" instead of "Trish Trish Trish!" which caused much laughter in the group and meant Trish had to stand in the middle to call on someone else. The whole experience had been very infantile Trish thought.

Doris caught her eye and smiled gently, as if to say, it would all be ok.

"Oh and the owl" Anthony added.

There was another snort of laughter from

Damon.

"Damon - you are the witch and narrator, " Anthony cut over Damon's snort,
diverting attention away from Trish.

Damon mumbled something that sounded
suspiciously like "for fecks sake."

"Doris, you will be Gretel and that leaves
Dylan as Hansel, " Anthony finished the
list quickly brushing past Damon's bad language.

Dylan felt his face go red. "Can't I work
the lights?" Dylan moaned.

"No" Anthony snapped. "Let's get started.
I think we should play a game."

"Working together, you have 5 seconds
to make me a square using just your bodies
- GO!" Anthony yelled

Trish jumped up and quickly got to work
moving each person into the position she

felt was correct. Dylan sat and refused to move. Damon shrugged Trish's hands from his shoulders as she attempted to get him to be a straight line.

"Don't touch me!" He growled.

"3, 2, and 1!" Anthony shouted "Let's see how you've done; well this is almost a square if you could just make the sides there Damon and Dylan- are you the middle? Very good. Now make me a house!"

"A house?!" the group chorused "But how...?"

"5!" Anthony started. Trish started again, busily trying to get the group into her perfect house positions.

Delius lay flat on the floor and was adamant he was a doormat, Doris became the door and Damon was the toilet - much to Trish's despair.

"Very good" cried Anthony. He continued to call out some more objects and creatures for the group to create.

Next came a read through of the script, a chance for people to play and find their characters. Damon was quite impressive as the witch.

"I'll just dress myself up so much that no one recognises me, " he explained.

After the morning session everyone was surprised with how hungry they'd become, when lunch was announced the group there was a genuine feeling of relief in the cast.

Chapter 3

Second Opinions

Anthony paced around the newly constructed stage and moved a cardboard screen back into the correct position.

He stared up at the sound and lighting booth as it overhangs the edge of the stage

"How did you think that went?" He shouted, neck tilted back.

"Pretty good...They're a good mix"

"Do you think so?" he asked as he moved towards the front seat of the Auditorium to pick up the newly written script and started to exit into an empty dressing room.

"THEY ARE EXACTLY THE SAME AS THE LAST CAST, YOU DINGUS!"

Anthony looked into a lightbulb festooned, full length mirror and answered like he was berating himself.

"Don't be stupid, they look nothing like them."

He collected a green cloak and wooden stick from the corner of the room and carefully folded the garment and placed both items into a store cupboard.

"Anthony, don't let this happen again, you've got to try and move on."

"I have moved on."

"This is the fifth time you've done Hansel and Gretel."

"So?'

"THIS YEAR ANTHONY! THIS YEAR!"

Anthony became agitated and moved quickly into a side room used for laundry and costumes and shut the door behind him.

"Alright! Alright! I just need to, I don't know, I just don't..."

He slumped into a chair and looked up at a tattered promotion poster for a show that happened before he arrived at the theatre. He closed his eyes.

" I understand, but you've got to try and get over this. It's too much pressure on yourself and this company. It's not going to be perfect Ant, but it will be good"

Anthony whispered to himself.

"Good is never enough though is it? Anyway!"

Anthony jumped up and recollected himself with a forced sense of gusto.

"Where are we at with it? What do you think?".

"It's fine; you need to just chill Anthony. I sense that you're very nervous. You don't want to have it repeated. I'm afraid it's going to happen again."

Anthony left the room and hastily made his way towards the green room.

"It's ridiculous! The notion that the whole place goes fruit bat crazy everytime I run this performance."

"It happens bro."

He opened the double doors into the green room where the actors were eating and chatting away.

"Right people! 10 minutes and we are back in rehearsal!".

He re-entered the stage and looked back up to the darkened booth.

"You know Bro. It's not that as bad as you think up here. It's comfortable and I don't miss you that much!"

"You're a right spoon."

"Only kidding. it's just that I'm fine with it. I'm all good."

"Don't, " Anthony looked away.

"At least I wouldn't have been cast as Dad every time you decided to do Hansel and Gretel."

Anthony shed a tear. "I do all this for you; I miss you. It was the happiest time of my life"

"Get over it dingus"

"Like I said, you're a spoon Alex"

Anthony wiped away his tears.

Chapter 4

Mental Blocking

"Why am I here, thought Damon, I'm not even it this scene. After two days of games and messing around we are finally doing something purposeful, and I'm not in it. Shouldn't the Witch be a woman? How did I end up with a girl's character?'

"Ok! Everyone on stage please, not you Damon, sorry, not everyone". Anthony is trying his best to bring some energy and focus to the now cast Hansel and Gretel company. As you can imagine there are some who are delighted with the roles they have received and some are equally perplexed or even devastated! Patricia is at this moment trying her best to calm the redness of eyes in the guest dressing room' backstage.

"Hansel, Gretel, Mother Father! This is the beginning of our play, let's make it clear. We will start with Hansel and Gretel playing and the Mother and Father talking. Remember where the audience are, they need to see your faces, and speak loud, the old lady at the back must be able to hear you!"

"I don't know what we're suppose to be doing, " moaned Dylan.

"We just play here, and they talk. Maybe you pretend you have a car or something and I will be reading a book... or we could throw a ball to each other, " suggested Doris.

"No balls on stage!" Anthony immediately regretted his words as the whole room burst out laughing

"Let's not do that then" smiled Doris as the rehearsal began.

Mother: "Husband, we can't afford to keep the children, they are useless, stupid and lazy. Let's take them to the forest and leave them there."

Father: "We can't do that, they are our kids. I actually kind of love them."

* * *

Everyone loved Doris. She was such an extraordinary teenager. You know how

33

people say "the youth of today, " if every kid was like Doris no one would complain. She looked after her siblings, fed them, took them to school, all the things that parents do normally.

"Mum is working very hard. And anyway, I don't mind. I love Tim and Tracy, they make me laugh all the time, and they are very well behaved."

Doris also worked several jobs. She was too young to have a well paid job but she walked dogs and helped in a cafe.

"It's not work, it's fun. I want to support mum and take some weight off her shoulders, and anyway, walking dogs is good for your health, and you can chat to other people with dogs. I like dogs, but we could never have one. And the coffee shop, it's a cosy little place, not very busy and it's run by my mum's friend so I get a proper work experience, it will be good for the future."

Where is the dad?' you might ask. He left them as soon as Tracy was born, over 7 years ago. And he doesn't care, he never came back.

"Dad... he got lost. It was maybe too much for him, I don't know... I don't think about it, there is no time. He is gone and that's it, why do you even bring this up?"

Doris was one of those kids that got on with everyone, all ages, all backgrounds. Her grandparents lived in a sheltered housing with other elderly people, and guess what? Doris was everyone's favourite granddaughter. She found time for everyone, played chess with 85 year old Mark, and painted the nails of 90 year old Elaine. How she found time for all that is anyone's guess.

"Why are you making it sound like it's a big deal? They have amazing stories and it's like a time travel or something. I learn so much from them and they give me cake."

* * *

"Gretel, I mean Doris wake up! Ok listen up...You are all supposed to be going through the forest now. Damon stop messing with your phone. Everyone you need to show respect to the people who are on the stage. They will be paying attention when it's your time. Damon, please can you come on stage and be a tree Remember this is a magical story nothing is as it seems. Perhaps as the Witch you have shape-shifted' in order to see what is going on in your woods" Anthony resisted jumping on to the stage in order to demonstrate how he wanted to cast to play their parts.

"Let them discover it for themselves" Anthony could feel Alex's hand on his shoulder to steady him.

Hansel: "Where are they taking us Gretel? It's not Saturday. And the weather is awful."

Dylan read the line in a very awkward robotic fashion, wanting the stage floor to open up and swallow him.

Gretel: "Maybe mum and dad want to spend some more time with us, look they have a basket, maybe we will have a picnic. Why are you so grumpy?"

Doris responded, Dylan was amazed how easily and naturally she could reel off her lines.

Hansel: "I'm not grumpy, I'm just cold,

" Dylan mumbled.

"Who wrote this play? This is rubbish!"

"We did. We can still change it if you want, " said Doris grinning at him.

* * *

Look at her. Doris will always listen to other people and try to understand, to make sure that they are fine. She forgets about herself. What do you want for yourself Doris?

"How do you mean? I want my mum to get some rest and I want Tim and Tracy to do well at school. I want my grandparents to feel well."

That is all for other people, what do you want for YOU?

* * *

"Good! Now kids go to sleep, parents

you leave them and you go off stage. Not yet! When they fall asleep, " called Anthony.

* * *

Doris doesn't even know what she wants. No dreams like other kids have. No time to dream.

"I don't have time to think about it."

If that helps, your mum would be happy if you did some things for yourself, why do you think she told you to come here?

"I will think about that when I get some time, promise."

Chapter 5

Playing House

Anthony brought Damon, Doris and Dylan into a small rehearsal studio which was completely empty, as blank as the first page of a new exercise book, and just as intimidating or inviting, depending on your disposition.

"First of all, congratulations on being cast in these three crucial roles.have any of you got any questions? Dylan, you look a bit shocked, but I know you can all do this. As I said to everyone this morning, there are no better or worse parts in our production, and absolutely everyone is as important as everyone else. That's the great thing about theatre, we are a company. we are a family" His voice became distant as if he had drifted off to some other place.

"Right... Who can tell me a point in the play where something is lost?"

Dylan begrudgingly pushed his hand into the air.

"Hold that thought?" Anthony looked around the group, "Damon, how about you?"

This was met with a now famous Damon glare', masking his feeling of rising panic. Doris came to his rescue.

"When Hansel and Gretel are trying to

get home."

She hadn't waited for Anthony to ask her and was shocked at her own certainty, or was it a new found confidence or sense of importance?. Anthony responded with a surprised smile and acknowledged this new version of Doris with approvingly raised eyebrows.

"Absolutely, and so I want you to go and share with each other your own real experiences of being lost'. Explore how you can use these experiences to help bring truth' to this moment on our stage right, off you go I'll be back in about 20 minutes to see how you are doing. Damon, I'd like you to direct the moments when Hansel and Gretel wake up and find themselves alone. Dylan and Doris you must help Damon discover why and how his character became so cruel and cunning."

He left the space.

The three of them looked at each other. Damon was surprised to hear his voice without any hint of sarcasm say " Ok, let's look at the lost stories who want's to go first?"

Anthony had left him with an audio recorder from the theatre, an expensive piece of kit that would never normally have been left in his charge. He carefully set up the mic and checked the levels. "Don't worry if you get bits wrong or make mistakes we can always edit it out later."

Doris smiled at him, it seemed she wasn't the only one who was acting differently today. Damon's reassurance made her feel brave. "I was lost once. It was before my siblings were born. My dad took me out and we went to the theme park. I stopped to look at prices coconut shy and when I turned around my dad was gone. I couldn't see him anywhere. I walked around looking for him but he just wasn't there. I started crying... I was very little then, and someone picked me up and took me to the information place or something, and they called my dad over the speakers in the park, he came to collect me, he was very angry with me... I wasn't sure if I was happy to see him, " Doris finished, still not sure how she felt about the whole experience.

*   *   *

As Doris shared her story a strange mist

descended over the world outside the theatre. A group of school children up from London were chatting noisily as they made their way through an old pottery museum. Clutching their souvenir pencils, rulers and magnets with names on, they got onto the school bus. But in a dark part of the pot bank a small voice was heard. "Hello, where has everyone gone?"

As the lone child walked further into the museum, searching for the others, he called out again this time with a strong Stoke accent. "Aye up Duck.. bin yer?"

*   *   *

Alex watched from behind the control

room. Damon was recording the lost stories and directing the lost children scenes. Alex watched, he knew the consequences that decisions made in the theatre would have on the outside world.

As he watched, Doris suggested that maybe the children could have a cat to guide them home, she laughed, "Maybe it should talk!".

What a headline that would be' thought Alex.

Patricia put her head to one side. "That's Alice in Wonderland".

"Oh yeah, ok let's sing a song about breadcrumbs, " said Doris.

Damon shot her a look, "I'm not singing."

Dylan had stopped listening and was thinking of a story his mother had told him when he was young and couldn't sleep because he'd lost Music Duck'. He had been about four years old and Music Duck' had been in his bed from the hour that he was born. They went everywhere together. It was their first holiday as a different kind of a family; Mum, Jim, Dylan and Music Duck of course, had been on. They had needed to run to catch the bus home and Music Duck had been left behind on the bench at the bus-stop. That night his mum told him a story about all the lost toys in the world travelling to a magic world where they played all day together and at night curled up with the children who had lost them, holding them close to help them sleep. Even at four he knew it was a made up story, but somehow the thoughts of Music Duck and all those other lost toys curled up together brought a little smile to his face as he drifted off to sleep.

"Come on you lot, Anthony will be back soon we need to crack on" Damon's voice brought Dylan back into the studio space and all three knuckled down to continue working on their scene.

It seemed like no time had passed as Anthony bounced back into the studio, with Alex right behind him as always. Clapping his hands together he said "Right everyone, hopefully you have come up with something and not just been chatting amongst yourselves."

The whole Hansel and Gretel company gathered and Damon's group performed their scenes back to the rest of the cast in the main auditorium. Their show-back' went well and the rest of the group really connected with the ideas they had presented. The three of them had "worked "like professionals" as Anthony liked to say.

It was the first time in his life that Damon had heard genuine spontaneous applause from his peers and adults and rather than brushing it aside as if it was nothing, Damon took it in and felt it deep inside his body. It was a good feeling.

Chapter 6

Behind the Curtain

A theatre always feels strange when the people leave and the lights are turned off. Shadows of the day can still be seen and felt around the auditorium and the sounds of lines being run, laughter and stillness, "places everyone please" and applause, resonate around the empty space.

Mike the security man said goodbye to what he thought was the last person from the Hansel and Gretel cast and began his usual rounds of the theatre, checking the windows, turning the lights out in each space as he checked it.

By this time Delius knew Mike's routine. His mum and dad had sent him and Patricia a text Running late. Pick u up at 6 not 5 hugs xoxoxo'. Patricia had gone to town to pick up a book from the library, so Delius decided it would be a laugh to hide in the theatre. Once he heard Mike going up stairs he snuck back into the theatre. He had sussed out the code for the keypads on day one, and now was his chance to use it.

The theatre was warm and still. The

empty seats congregated in a circle, anticipating, expecting. The safety lights around the drum created an intermittent orange glow. Delius sat down on the top of the steps looking down at the stage. He replayed in front of his eyes the scenes they had practised today and and found that without too much effort he could hear the voices of characters, Damon and Doris, as the witch and Gretel, Patricia arguing with Dylan...

"Mum is dying."

To Delius' ears Dylan's voice echoed round the theatre bouncing off every surface merging with itself, sometimes like a whisper coming from behind him and then flying in from the centre of the grid high above the stage.

"Mam yn marw" whispered Delius. He

knew it was true. He often heard truths which were unspoken. Dylan's mother would die soon and there was nothing to be done about it, she was moving to another place. Delius had glimpsed this place he was not afraid. He remembered the voices.

"Bodwch un bach dewr. Be brave little one."

"They did all right today didn't they" said Anthony who had entered the theatre downstage left'.

Delius quickly hid himself behind a seat. Anthony had his notes from the day's re-hearsals and was re-setting the stage ready for the technical rehearsal that would start tomorrow promptly at 10.00am. As Anthony walked around he was talking about each of the company in turn and looking for reassurance that the casting decisions he had made had been the right ones.

"You've cast yourself as Hansel again little bro, the lost kid, the tragic kid, the child filled with"

Delius could hear a second voice but could not yet see who Anthony was talking to.

A strange mist like low cloud in the mountains began to fill the empty space and the sound of rain grew louder. Delius saw dark shapes emerging as the stage now appeared to be flooded with water. Anthony was wading up to his waist reaching out to who his face was filled with anguish as the words he was screaming never entered this world.

"You can see me, " said Alex, kind face, sad eyes, sweet smile.

"Yes" said Delius without a hint of worry

or fear. He had come to accept the colours and voices shapes and sounds that surrounded him, but mostly he was not afraid because they had met before.

In that ruined castle the seven year old Delius had been comforted by this same kind-faced boy. He had learned to listen to the stones who spoke the language of the ancients. "Bodwch un bach dewr" both Alex and Delius said, not out loud but each could hear the others voice.

It was Delius's turn to help Alex, he went down into the lake that had formed on the stage and walked towards Anthony. At last Anthony's need to take hold of the outstretched hands of another was fulfilled as he took hold of Delius and held him close. The pair of them stood centre stage as the storm receded and dark shapes retreated and Alex turned and left.

"What are you doing here!"

Anthony quickly let go of Delius and held him in a neutral way' with his hands on both shoulders. He was looking at Delius to see if there was anything there that hinted at what he might have just seen. Delius was as laid back as ever not giving a single thought away with his words. "Mum's going to be late so I'm just hanging about, can I help with anything for tomorrow?"

Anthony heard the words of his brother in his heart be brave little one' and said, "come on then; we're starting with the fattening up the kids scene' so we need to make sure that we can fit Dylan in the cage..."

"He's smaller than me even though I'm only ." Delius stopped remembering Patricia's warning about his age.

Chapter 7

The Magic of Theatre

Dylan and Doris had decided to travel home together as they lived not too far away and in the same direction. It was a crisp night, the leaves danced in the wind and the street lights blinked into life. Trying to keep up with Dylan was proving a difficulty for Doris. Dylan had borrowed her bike and was standing on his pedals intermittently as he tried to keep his balance. He was also doing the odd wheelie much to Doris's annoyance. Doris was having to walk particularly fast to keep up and her shins were starting to hurt.

"I thought you were going to walk me home, not have me chase you down the street." panted Doris.

"Sorry, I'm struggling to keep my balance. What do you think of that Anthony? He's really starting to do my head in! Not sure I can be bothered to do this much more. I might not come in tomorrow."

"Don't be doing that! We've just had our characters sorted out and you're Hansel!"

"and.." said Dylan, his mind flicked to the beeping machines which hung around his mum's head.

"Well I'm Gretel aren't I?....don't throw me under the bus!...Anyhow, I think you've been doing really well this week, " Doris said honestly, she was able to make these words sound comforting and Dylan felt a tinge of guilt.

"That's like saying you're good in goals'..." Dylan snapped, pushing the guilt away. He did not have the energy to feel guilty as well as everything else right now.

"You're good in goals?" questioned Doris.

"You know.....its something you say to people when you really don't want to go in goals...Because no one wants to go in goals....cuz it's rubbish!....And no one wants to be Hansel or Gretel or any other stupid character in this play...cuz that's naff as well." Dylan had stopped to give Doris time to catch up. He swung his leg off the bike and began to push it in the direction they were walking.

"Well I'm excited by it and it's going pretty well...I think it's going to be good. I genuinely think that you're good and it's going to be good, you need to be able to tell yourself that...and stop being a martyr!" said Doris, thankful that he had slowed down.

"Yer what?"

"I'm only joshin'...Anyway, you better turn up tomorrow!" laughed Doris as she grabbed the handlebars of her bike and jumped on effortlessly.

"Where you going?"

"I live on this street down at the bottom end, " called Doris from over her shoulder.

"I live on this Street! Number 37, " said Dylan.

"Number 248... cool, we can walk in to-morrow, " Doris waved and began to head off.

Dylan had started to think about his evening, he would be going to the hospice like he did every night, to eat his dinner by his mum, chat to her and tell her about his day. This had become almost normal for him now. The nurses that looked after her were so warm and compassionate that he had stopped feeling awkward sitting there.

"She can hear you-you know - why not have a chat with her, read her something. She will be as bored as you are!" Gaynor had chuckled at him one afternoon. She was a large woman who seemed to make the room feel lighter when she entered it.

Dylan was suddenly pulled into the present as all around him something bizarre happened. All the street lights started to go out two by two, simultaneously at both sides of the street and all away along the road into the distance. like a landing strip gone wrong. As his sight adjusted, the cats eyes started to reflect down the centre of the street.

I hope it's not a blackout, ' thought Doris, I'm supposed to do the cooking tonight.'

Further on down the road. Mr Shnizzlewitz at No. 89 was listening to the local radio.

The Reporter chimed ....residents have said this is the fourth time in as many days where neighbours have been "acting" strangely out in the street.'

The voice of a local resident bumbled

through the speakers of the radio "Well, I'd seen both Miss Frank and Big John from just over chatting in rhyming couplets to each other from across the street on Monday! They were directly under the lamps and they didn't stop until they'd done the whole of Act 1 from Richard the Third...I think they were playing multiple roles at some points."

"And there was 6 of em' last night re-enacting the murder of Julius Caesar. There was one guy who waited a full 45 mins in silence to act out a scene where he just went "Aye"...or summat like that.... then exited stage left....which was down the driveway to his house"

"These strange occurrences coupled with some of the other inexplicable series of events across Stoke-On-Trent has lead to a local committee requesting that the council check the water supply for contamination." continued the reporter.

"As well as people acting out Shakespeare at sundown under street spotlights there have been reports of overnight obesity. Spontaneous applause and canned laughter during incidental and witty one liners in everyday conversations have also been reported. More disturbingly...people are complaining of getting lost in urban forests only to wake up in the city centre the following morning."

"And finally...an old lady went to the Ear Nose and Throat clinic claiming her Tabby cat called Busta Rhymes' had spoken to her to say thank you for feeding her Is this another connected event? Maybe not....'

Chapter 8

Sugar-Coated Cage

"Places please!" Anthony called.

The cast wandered onto the stage, Dylan and Doris stepped into their cage. Damon grabbed his cloak and cackled. The gingerbread house was nearly finished, the cardboard set was sprinkled with liquorice swirls and large jelly babies in an assortment of colours. The icing roof was a bright white and the floor was paved with large jelly beans. It looked like a level you might find in a game or app where sweets fall from the sky.

Dylan mumbled as he crouched on the floor. He would much rather be anywhere else, but at least they weren't playing stupid drama games.

"Whats up?" smiled Doris.

"Oh nothing. Can't remember my lines." Dylan lied. It was partly true, he had read the script to his Mum last night.

Doris pulled a crinkled page from her pocket, took the gum she had been chewing and used it as Blu Tack, attaching the script to the inside of the cage so Anthony couldn't see. "It's a sweetie house so gum for Blu Tack is probably better, " Doris grinned.

"Poke your finger through the cage boy - let me feel how fat you've gotten, " crowed Damon, peering through the bars and giving Dylan a broad grin.

Dylan closed his eyes wishing very much that he wasn't there, he pushed his finger through the wobbly cage bars secured on the floor by the stage weights. Dylan felt a warm hand clasped around his finger.

*   *   *

Dylan, opened his eyes, his mother lay silent in the bed in front of him. Her hand gently holding his finger. He looked at his mum; her face now pale and peaceful. She had lost her youth through the cancer, new worry lines chiselled on her forehead replaced the laugh lines that he remembered from birthdays, Christmas or lazy Saturdays watching Dylan and his brother Jim playing football in the garden.

Jim was softly sobbing beside him, neither of them had done much crying. His mum had been sick for a long time, they had gotten used to it. It was their normal'. She had cooked chicken fajitas; Dylan's favourite meal, the night she had told them the cancer had spread to her brain. It had been pretty quick after that. She had been in the hospice for the last few weeks.

Dylan felt the warm tears drip off his chin. It shouldn't have been this way -

she wasn't supposed to get sick, she was meant to be here to look after him, and pester him to do his homework or tidy his room, complain about the grass stains on his football kit and tell him off for playing computer games at 1am. She was meant to live; to watch him grow up.

The doctor entered the private room where they were sitting and spoke some quiet words to his brother. Jim nodded. Dylan knew what them meant. The machines would be turned off. His mum would die. This was the end. Dylan's life would never be the same, how would he cope? Dylan knew it had to happen, but he desperately wanted one more minute. She had been in such pain those last few days, her face contorted, whimpering, but now her face was soft, she made no sound.

The doctor seemed to float behind the bed, everything was a haze. Dylan wanted to cry out "No! Just one more minute - please!" but no sound came. The machines beeping around the bed fell silent, the comforting rise and fall of his mum's breathing began to gently slow.

"It's just a matter of waiting now." the doctor said softly. "It could take a while - your Mum is a fighter. But she has lots of pain relief and we have made her as comfortable as possible."

Dylan hated that phrase, Comfortable as possible, ' what did that even mean? Dylan was forced to leave by the nurses when the last bus left the hospital. "Go home, and get some rest - we will call you if there is any change."

Gaynor had gently pushed both boys

out of their chairs and waved them onto the bus. Dylan knew he couldn't do anything to help his Mum now. Nothing would change the inevitable.

*   *   *

"Dylan?"

Who was that?

"Dylan?"

Was that the doctor? Or Jim?

Dylan could hear his name, something was pulling him back to the present.

"Dylan! It's your line! For goodness sake everyone - the show is tomorrow! Can we focus please!" Anthony moaned from the seats in the audience.

"What time is it?" Anthony asked looking to his left. "3.30?" he nodded to
the empty seat beside him. "Right well,
I think we can have a break. Take 5 everyone." Anthony wiped his brow, feeling
anxious.

Chapter 9

"Nothing good ever happens in Wales"

"I can't believe we've been cast as Mother and Father! I mean it's a terrible decision, I mean we're brother and sister oh my days this play is going to be a disaster"

Patricia was almost in a perfect melt down. All her life she had been used to being in the starring role, after all that was the least that was expected of a child of two successful litigating barristers. "I mean we're too young to play parents. It's not like we even see anything of mum and dad to base it on." She was on the verge of tears.

Delius but his arm around his little-big sister and gave her a hug. "You are like the best mum in the world Trish, I know you shouldn't have to be, but I always feel safe when you're around. I know that you will always stick by me and that you are always filling in the gaps that mum and dad leave. It's not even their fault really, it's just the way they are.... Driven."

* * *

Both remembered Delius being left behind on a primary school trip. He was only seven, he was excited it was his first school trip. They had gone to the ruins of Dolwyddelan Castle in Blaenau Ffestiniog, Delius had drifted into one of his games in his head' as his dad used to say. "I don't know where he's come from" his mother would say "He's not like any of the rest of us you should send him back!" Patricia regretted those words as she realised that he little brother was not on the coach which had brought all the other children back. She had watch each excited face beaming with joy to be reunited with their parents after the adventures of the day. She looked behind every seat and eventually sat down on the steps of the coach and wailed in despair as her little heart broke at the thought of never seeing her little brother again.

Mr Boote had tried to console her as he tried in vain to get hold of her parents. The police in Ffestiniog were called and even mountain rescue dispatched as the dark storm clouds descended on the ruins. When the police had found Delius and brought him to school, Patricia held Delius in the back of Mr Boote's car all the way back home. Mr Boote gave their parents a proper ticking off. Delius could unexplainably speak Welsh.

*   *   *

Damon was turning into a seriously excellent director and together the cast created a scene which really put the world to right. No longer in the end of the story would the witch be burned in the oven and sent in a plume of purple smoke up the chimney, but would instead become a cherished pet, a dark furred cat that could speak to humans. And mum and dad recognised the error of their ways and decided that nothing was more important, (not even their glittering careers) than their rather marvelous children.

Patricia completely forgot about her earlier dismay and threw herself totally into the role of Mother'. Delius and Damon (as the Witch and Father) had created a fantastic sub-genre rap, which was like a mash up of Kate Tempest and Kanye West

The last day of rehearsal was over. Delius

and Trish left the theatre and moved straight to the carpark, but mum's car wasn't there. "Call her. She's probably stuck in traffic... as always." Delius prodded Trish. His phone never had any battery and even if it did he would often leave it at home.

Trish hunted for her phone in her bag. "I have a message from her, wait. She's not coming, she was on her way but got stuck in traffic and she said she will be late for the meeting so she is saying we should get a bus." Trish read the message, throwing the phone back in her bag she snorted "This is ridiculous, we don't know the area, how we suppose to find the way?! She says we can wait but it will take her an hour and a half to get here!"

"Where do you need to go?" Damon was leaning against the wall rolling a fag.

"Home, " Delius said, although he was quite happy sitting in the carpark watching the leaves fall around them.

"He doesn't know where we live silly. We live in Ashley."

"That's miles away. You could walk with me, it's the right direction and maybe we could check how you can get home on my mum's computer, " suggested Damon. He immediately regretted this suggestion.

"Thanks that would be great, " Trish smiled. "Surprise surprise our parents aren't here. As usual."

"I'm not even gonna bother buying them tickets to see the show as it will be a waste of money." Delius retorted.

"It'll be just like last parents evening - I sat outside my classroom alone waiting for either one of them to show and they never did. In the end Mr Coates had to drive me home." sighed Trish.

"Well I haven't even told my dad about their being a show. I can see him now "You're being a witch? That's a girl's role! Who is the director I'll have him for making me son wear a dress!" Damon mimed smacking someone in the face and taking a swig of beer.

Trish laughed Damon dropped the act quickly - that was too much information to give out in one go.

As they headed home Damon listened to Delius and Trish's retelling of countless birthdays and Christmases when one or both parents had to rush off to work, how they hadn't made the costume for the end of year show, how they had been left in the cold waiting for the moment of free time that their mum or dad had in their hectic work schedules or dinner parties or court cases.

As the tread of their steps fell into rhythm with each other Damon wondered what he would find at home. His dad passed out on the sofa, the finished whiskey bottle in his hand, fresh bruises on his mum's cheek. He never brought people home, but then again he never really spent time with anyone outside of the house either. His stomach turned, he looked at Trish and Delius - what would they think? Would they say anything to anyone else? Well, even if they did he would handle it - the way he handled everything else, knocking people down with a flick of his tongue. He was quite proud of how quickly he could hone in on someone's weakness and insecurity and cut them down. But letting people into his house, letting them see this part of his world - that was new.

They walked through the front garden squeezing past the overgrown hedge and stepped over the broken wooden gate that his dad had fallen through one night after a particularly heavy evening in the pub. The front door was wide open and Damon could see that his dad was out. His massive frame was hard to miss when he was home sprawled across the sofa. "Hello - Mum?" Damon called, glancing at the other two. Delius, Damon was pleased to see did not bat an eyelid at the state of the living room. Trish hovered by the doorway.

"I'm in the kitchen, " his Mum chirped.

"I have brought my friends from the

theatre, " Damon called.

"You have friends?" she said as she poked her head round the kitchen doorway. Her joking smile transformed into a genuine glow as she saw Delius and Trish standing in the living room.

"They need to check how to get to Ashton, can they use your computer?" said Damon, his eyes darting to the stairs desperate to make this encounter as quick as possible.

"Your dad's not in, " Damon's Mum said, noticing Damon's anxiety. "My laptop is in the case by the window - help yourself. Would you like to stay for dinner? Ashton is miles away - There is plenty for everyone."

"We don't want to cause a problem, " said Trish nervously.

"That is not a problem, aren't you hungry?"

"I'm hungry, " said Delius

"Delius!" Trish scolded, "That would be very nice, thank you."

The house was a bit messy and smelled of cigarettes but it didn't matter because Ms. Andrews prepared beans on toast for everyone and they all sat on the sofa. They chatted about the day, Damon's Mum was excited about the play and asked all sorts of questions which made Damon blush "Mum shurrup!"

Trish stopped caring about the state of the room and the smell of cigarettes and relaxed into the care and warmth that Damon's mum showed to each child. She busily offered them more beans or toast and the three were full up by the time

Delius and Trish's dad arrived to pick them up. He honked the horn from outside, and thanked Ms. Andrews through the open car window with an air of importance and the look of a bad smell under his nose. The pair dived into the back as he barked "Quickly! I have a skype meeting in 15 minutes!" and with that he turned the car around and sped off.

Chapter 10

Unusual Goings On

If you looked around the shop it was just like any other morning in a superstore. Bored people going about their daily lives, filling time between dropping kids off at school and collecting them again, or quickly grabbing a sandwich before all the best ones

were taken and all that is left is a sad looking cheese sandwich that's been well handled by disinterested passersby. No one in
the shop seemed to have noticed the out
of the ordinary events surrounding them.
A mist seemed to hang in the air.

Up by the bread was a lady. She looked
sadly into her purse and sighed. It appeared that for the second time this week
she had forgotten to get cash out. She quietly cursed herself and her forgetful mind,
and began to walk toward the exit. She
became aware of the music being played
through the shop. It started to fill the air
around her, a tune so melancholy it would
bring even the happiest of people to their
knees with despair.

Even though she had never heard the
tune before, she began to sing, the words

came so naturally to her it seemed like a well rehearsed aria that was being performed on the Royal Opera House stage. She saw the crowd, and heard the applause as she sang "Twice in one Week.It is Ri-di-cu-lous. How can someone be so MEEEEEK." She went for the high note.

Other people in the supermarket looked up from their daily shop, they didn't share in the same fantasy. A man grabbed a loaf and with a pained look on his face swiftly moved on to the milk aisle. He wished he had been further away before the high note, now he knew how Simon Cowell felt. Sorry, it's a no from me, ' he thought as he scurried away.

Later, Joe was making his way back to his terraced house from the newsagent around the corner. He was more hurried than usual, and was slightly exhausted by his excursion. Mrs. Teaks came to speak to him but he gave her a quick wave and hurried on by. He didn't stop to chat with neighbours like he usually did.

"Samantha, Samantha!" he cried as he dashed in through the front door. "Samantha!" he called again. "What is it Joe?" she pottered into the front room with no hint of the urgency that was implied by his calls. She had been absent mindly watering the plants, they didn't really need watering but it did fill the time.

"Have you seen this?" he said waving the newspaper about like a windmill. "Have you bloody seen this? The world is mad, I'm telling you Samantha, mad." Samantha carried on watering plants. "Hmmm" she said uninterested.

"Woman has talking cat!" How does a
bloody cat talk? Spotlights! Spotlights!
Appearing all over the place. It's aliens,
I'm telling you aliens!" exclaimed Joe. Samantha sighed "You always say it's aliens Joe,
it was aliens when your glasses went missing, it was aliens when your car wouldn't
start, " she trailed off.

Joe sat down in his armchair, disap-
pointed in Samantha's reaction. In his day
a man could come home tell his wife he
thought it was aliens and she would agree
with him no questions asked. The world
had changed, for the better of course. He
opened the newspaper and on page two
was a long article about a woman singing
in Tesco who was discovered by a talent
agent. Apparently singing in tune Is so
last year- now it's all about the lyrics'. Joe

tutted put the paper down and went to make a cup of tea.

Chapter 11

The Show Must Go On

It's always frantic the day of the show. Nerves start to take over, visits to the toilet increase and the what ifs' start. What if i forget my lines?, What if I fall over?, What if my costume doesn't fit? The theatre is alive there are people all over the place, coats have been abandoned on the back of seats, ladders are on the stage, cardboard sets are being repaired. With all the people and the fuss it goes unnoticed that someone is missing. Anthony is in the corner using his arms to make a point, Alex unnoticed by his side. Patricia is quietly studying her lines, while Damon is struggling with a green wig.

A shout of "places everyone" and a scattering of people dash to various locations around the stage. Delius is the last to get into place, and Doris fusses over his costume. She turns to her right expecting to see Dylan appear at her side ready for their entrance. He isn't there. She looks around urgently trying to spot him in the darkened auditorium, she rushes to the other side of the stage hoping that he is on the wrong side again. He isn't there. Doris shouts out "Where is Dylan?" the others look to each other with a puzzled look.

"Has anyone actually seen him this morning?" says Patricia.

Alex looks up and asks Anthony "Have you heard from him today?" Anthony checks his phone for messages a feeling of guilt comes over him as he realises that he hasn't noticed that someone was missing.

Anthony starts to panic, "Why Alex, does this always happen. People will be here and there won't be a Hansel!. It's ruined again!"

"He will turn up, " Alex says trying to be reassuring.

"You will have to play Hansel, it's the only answer." Anthony says staring at Alex.

"You and I both know that's not possible Anthony, " Alex looks across at the worried faces now gathered in the middle of the stage. "They need you to tell them it will be fine."

"Okay guys....Don't worry. If it comes to it I can step in." They all look up at Anthony slightly aghast assessing if he is being serious. This wasn't quite what Alex had in mind.

"Are you being serious?" says Patricia.

"Yes he's being serious Dish, " says Doris incredulous.

"But isn't he too old?" whispers Damon.

"This is going to be rubbish. I'm so upset! I don't want to do this, " Patricia was frantic. There was so much noise from the gathered group, no one could hear anything anymore, just a mixed up chatter. Delius sees Anthony who seems to be talking to himself in the corner, he wonders if he is trying to remember Hansel's lines.

"We need to work as a team, " said Damon, his voice carried above the din, surprising the group. They all stopped their panicked chatter and stared at him. "Well, you know, people are coming to this whatever happens. I don't want to look stupid."

They stared at Damon, dumbfounded, for the first time he said something that they could all agree with, something that isn't a joke. "He's right you know" said Doris, "whatever happens with Dylan, we have to put on a play."

"So what can we do?" Damon said, trying to take charge of the situation.

"Maybe the narrator could add Hansel's lines in?" suggested Doris meekly.

"It's a start, " said Damon.

Patricia looked worried, glancing around the room. "We only have small parts, " Trish vocalised the worry that had been eating at her "Mum and Dad will think that we are not good enough and that's why we didn't get the Hansel and Gretel parts, I guess it's still better than being a Witch. They won't come anyway, I'm sure there will be something more important."

Doris smiled and put her arm around Trish. "I would love it if Mum, Tracy and Tim, Nan and Granddad could come, and Mark and Elaine, Pam from the cafe. I would really, really like that." Doris said, she knew it was very unlikely as everyone was busy with their own lives, hospital appointments and jobs."

"I just home my dad doesn't come" mumbled Damon absentmindedly pulling a thread which hung from his sleeve. He looked up and saw Doris's caring eyes looking at him, not wanting to show weakness he quickly changed the attention to Dylan's absence.

Everyone had the same collective dread in the pit of their stomach, what if all their hard work was for nothing? Only Delius seemed immune from this feeling. "It will be fine" he said. Everyone hoped it to be true, but they did not feel it.

Chapter 12

The Final Curtain

The door banged and Anthony appeared in the doorway looking overwrought, there in front of him was Dylan. He was standing in a bright white light looking down at his feet, there were what looked like clouds above Dylan's head and heavy rain was falling from them, right there in the foyer, soaking the carpet.

"I can't do it." Dylan shouted through the storm. "I can't find my way home."

Alex appeared silently beside Anthony and handed him a large umbrella, as quickly as he appeared Alex disappeared into the darkness. The crying lament of a distant violin could be heard through the pouring rain and Anthony could see that Dylan was crying.

The water started to flood around their feet, Anthony tried to wade towards Dylan. The rain and wind was lashing in Anthony's face making it a struggle to walk, holding his hands up to stop the torrent he called out to Dylan his voice drowned out by the storm.

"There is no home for me anymore - no

one there. I don't see the point in anything. I can't see my future. I'm stuck." Dylan whispered, the howl of the wind and the rain did not drown out his voice which seemed to reverberate from every wall in the foyer of the theatre. Anthony was edging closer to Dylan, he had no idea how to get to him, how to help or what to say.

The outside world looked strange through the window of the theatre, there was no rain, but things were beginning to getting out of control. The football stadium had now turned into a giant cake and been renamed the "Britannia Cakey-Yum". Wedgewood was purely made of battenberg and the Emma Bridgewater factory was a giant steaming, nicely decorated, pot of witch's brew. The population was becoming fattened up at an accelerated rate, an obesity crisis was looming. The local mayor gave a speech asking for calm, but even she had succumbed to the strange events. "I ask the people to use their loaf. It's all fun and games lentil someone gets hurt! This turnip of events is a bit munch. We will leave no scone unturned, to end this rices.. I mean crisis"

Back in the foyer Dylan was drenched, he was shivering in the spotlight which seemed miles from where Anthony was desperately crawling.

"I can't help!" cried Anthony deflated.

Alex popped up beside him, the rain wasn't touching him, but was repelled off as if they were protected by a force field. "Alex, it's no use I can't do it." Anthony groaned.

Silently Alex lifted Anthony without a

strain, as if there was no weight to him. He smiled at Anthony, "Remember when we were boys? Remember how you ..."

The realisation dawned and Anthony knew what it was he needed to do. He looked at Dylan, seeing the same pain he lived with day in, day out etched across the boys face.

"Dylan, I understand. Your world has stopped right now, there is no easy way out of how you are feeling, but perhaps that's right. Losing someone is not easy, I don't think we would want it to be. We want the world to be still, people to stop, just pause for a moment. That our loss should shudder through their worlds. But it doesn't. It doesn't touch them and that doesn't touch our grief. But it will get easier. You will never forget your mum, the times you shared, but this pain will lessen. Sadly we cannot hide from our feelings and we cannot hide from life. This performance just like the world around you is going to continue, you can join us or you can hide. It's your choice."

The rain had slowed to a shower, the grey skies still loomed overhead. Anthony looked over at Alex, he was standing with a woman. She had a warm kind face and she was beaming at Dylan.

Dylan looked up and noticed the woman beaming at him, his eyes filled with tears. "I don't want to do this Mum, I don't know how."

Dylan's Mum simply beamed at him, the room filled with warmth, the clouds disappeared, the sodden carpet drained of all moisture and Dylan noticed that shining silver pebbles had appeared at his feet, leading him into the auditorium. Dylan stared at the pebbles. He nodded and after glancing up at Anthony he took a deep breath, his heart still breaking in his chest, together they started to follow the pebbles.

Suddenly there standing right in front of them were Alex and Dylan's Mum. Alex leant forward and embraced Anthony, Dylan noticed they were both crying. Tears of sadness, tears of relief. Dylan looked at his mum, she enveloped him in her arms. Dylan felt her strength, her joy and he knew she was not in any pain anymore.

"Be brave little one, " Dylan's Mum whispered softly to Dylan as she faded from his sight, the words ringing gently in Dylan's ears like a lullaby she used to sing to him in the middle of a dark night.

*   *   *

He didn't want to face the rest of the
group but there was no escape.

"Sorry I'm late, " said Dylan.

"How could you leave us like that? This
is so irresponsible, and so selfish, " Patricia
yelled at him.

"Important thing is that he is here, can
we just get on with it?" Damon said.

The group agreed.

"Places everyone!" Anthony said, the
group gathered themselves in the wings,
"Here we go!" Doris said excitedly.

Chapter 13

All the World's a Stage

Anthony gave a deep sigh of relief as the curtain fell.

"It's over, pretty good in the end wasn't it?"

Anthony turned to find that Alex was no longer there by his side. He was taken aback. Applause washed over him like white noise for the briefest of moments and then he realised. He turned back around and made his way backstage.

"Well done everybody. That was really good, you should be proud of what you've achieved in 5 days."

The group erupted in cheers and no one heard Anthony's praise. Quickly they changed out of their costumes, with cries of "Where's my shoe?!" "Has anyone seen my sock?!" thrown in amongst the rush to get out and see the audience. Trish banged on the door of the boys changing room

"Delius! Where are you? Mum and Dad are here - they saw the whole thing!" Trish barged into the changing room and frogmarched Delius out to see his parents, almost to prove to him they were there.

One by one the cast emerged sheepishly from the dressing rooms, each time the door opened a cheer echoed through the ever emptying room. Doris was surprised to see that her Mum was there, looking exhausted but very proud. Her younger siblings ran to her as she emerged from the changing room with yells of "You were great!" Even her grandparents were there with some of the elderly residents from the sheltered housing who all agreed it was the best play they had ever seen.

Dylan felt very strange in the dressing room. He and Damon were the last to leave. There was a knock on the changing room door and Jim poked his head round.

"Alright mate?" Jim asked Dylan. "That was great. Are you ready to go?"

Dylan nodded, he hadn't wanted to be

there at the start of the week, but now, he somehow did not want to leave.

"You coming?" he asked.

"Yeah, I suppose." Damon responded.

They left the changing room and went into the foyer of the theatre.

"Damon! There you are, your Mum and Dad are waiting for you." Trish called from the other side of the room, grinning from ear to ear whilst posing for the photo her mum was taking.

Damon searched the room, and there in the corner was his Mum and Dad. Taking a deep breath he walked towards them.

"There you are! Well done!" his mum called. Damon's dad was standing with his back to him.

"Is there a bar here?" his dad asked, looking around. "Oh aye up Damon, you did alright son. I'm impressed; I didn't know you could do that."

Damon grinned. He looked around the room at all the other cast members enjoying the praise from their family members and congratulating each other.

"Hey Anthony?!" Doris' voice emerged from the gaggle of family and friends "When are we doing this again?"

Anthony had been watching the families' excitement, he breathed a sigh, the tension of the past week seemed to fall away, he massaged his neck with his hand. He had a mixture of joy, relief, and sadness. This was no longer the sadness that radiated from every ounce of him, but an acknowledgement that things would be different now, Alex had gone. It did not feel explosive anymore but matter of fact.

"We will do something for Christmas - I was thinking we could do Treasure Island, " Anthony said, "What do you think?"

"Ace! I'm Blackbeard!" shouted Damon.

There was a general consensus that that was a good idea, Trish was pleased that she had already read the book and knew plenty of knots which would be very useful for realistic set dressing.

As the families went home, still elated from the night's events, Anthony gathered his things and turned off the lights in the theatre.

"You all finished?" Mike the security guard asked. "It go well?"

"Yeah, it went really well." said Anthony waving to Mike as he left the room.

"Finished." Anthony sighed as the door

closed behind him. Treasure Island would be a whole new adventure, he thought as he started to make his way home.

Looking around the streets now, you would never know the strange events that had taken place over the last few days. People walked around like nothing had happened. The stadium was a stadium again, the battenburg had gone and cats had stopped speaking to old ladies. The supermarket song lady no longer had a top ten hit and people went about their daily business. It was unclear if people remembered what they had been through or if they had chosen to forget. Sometimes things are best left alone, after all what if it was aliens?
THE END

Our Authors

Pippa Church

Pippa is a Practitioner at the New Vic Theatre, she spends her time making lanterns, puppets and large scale parade items. She can often be found covered in paint of some description and doesn't own any clothes without holes in. She often waits far too long to have her hair cut.

Her largest accomplishment is staying alive until 30.75 years old.

Brendan Davies

Once voted the World's youngest man at age 16, I have been a great advocate for my own sense of worthiness. I am also a humble person who can work on my own initiative as well as in a team setting. Not on this occasion however.....

It has been an excruciatingly delightful experience. One which I wouldn't like to try again...as it would tarnish my memory of this struggle.

I have collaborated with some of the greatest minds...so this was interesting to work with some of my work colleagues.

In conclusion. We turned up. We wrote it. It happened. And no one could say it didn't.

In truth I have really enjoyed it! It has given me the bug to do more creative writing and will be using the ideas we've been given to help inform my own writing.

Thank you!

Sue Moffat

This is Sue's first attempt at writing a novel. She has written many lists (which she sometimes rewrites several times a day reordering their priority as the day progresses) and reports and funding bids. She has been known to contribute to academic papers including, it has been rumoured, 4* Journals. She is a violinist when playing Bach and a fiddler with Mood Food Ceilidh Band. Her best productions are Sam, Ellie, Lotte and Tom.

Rachel Reddihough

At the start of the week I was completely befuddled by the whole experience. I was overwrought with a sense of trepidation and ennui. This subsided somewhat after I read the whole of Roget's Thesaurus and was able to accentuate what I was scribing.

Julianna Skarzynska

Can eat a bulb of garlic and a spoon of cinnamon.

I wrote a book once and then realised it was written before by someone else.

Writing in English is probably not my biggest strength but it was an interesting experience.

I'm glad there was a design the cover' task.

I have other virtues too.

Printed in Great Britain
by Amazon